Oh, Bother!
SOMEONE'S
FIBBING!

Story by Betty Birney
Illustrated by Sue DiCicco

A GOLDEN BOOK • NEW YORK
Western Publishing Company, Inc., Racine, Wisconsin 53404

© 1991 The Walt Disney Company. All rights reserved. Printed in the U.S.A. No part of this book may be reproduced or copied in any form without written permission from the copyright owner. GOLDEN, GOLDEN & DESIGN, GOLDENCRAFT, A GOLDEN BOOK, and A GOLDEN LOOK-LOOK BOOK are registered trademarks of Western Publishing Company, Inc. Library of Congress Catalog Number: 90-85680 ISBN: 0-307-12636-6/ISBN: 0-307-62636-9 (lib. bdg.) MCMXCIV

It was a quiet afternoon in the Hundred-Acre Wood, where
Winnie the Pooh and his good friend Piglet were gathering
haycorns.

Suddenly they heard a loud rumbling noise. "Roarrrr!"

"Oh, bother," said Pooh. "I have a rumbly in my tumbly.
That means it's time for some honey."

"Buzz-Buzzzz," came another noise. A bee landed right on
Pooh's nose.

Pooh was happy to see the bee. "If I follow the bee, I will find honey," he said.

"I'll get one of your honey pots to put it in," said Piglet.

"Make sure it's my lucky green honey pot!" Pooh called to his friend.

At Pooh's house, Piglet found the lucky green honey pot.
Then he hurried back to meet Pooh.

But the lucky green honey pot was so tall, Piglet could not see where he was going. He tripped over a vine and CRASH! The pot smashed to pieces.

"Oh, dear! Pooh will be sad because I broke his lucky honey
pot," Piglet thought. "Maybe he won't want to be my friend
anymore."

As Piglet thought about life without his friend Winnie the
Pooh, he felt very sad.

Then he had an idea. He began to dig a hole.

Just as Piglet finished burying the broken pieces of the honey pot, Pooh arrived.

"What kept you, Piglet?" said Pooh. "Did you find my honey pot?"

Piglet knew he had to tell Pooh something. So he decided to tell a fib.

"Oh, Pooh! It was terrible! A Heffa-Heffa-Heffalump broke into your house and stole your lucky green honey pot!" he explained.

Pooh was shocked. "We must warn our friends in the Hundred-Acre Wood."

"M-must w-we?" Piglet asked nervously.

Pooh and Piglet told Rabbit about the Heffalump.
"Heffalumps stealing honey pots!" exclaimed Rabbit. "Why
next, they'll be stealing my lettuce. Something must be done!"

"Did you really see the Heffalump?" Rabbit asked.
"With my very own eyes," Piglet fibbed again.
Rabbit called to Owl, who was flying overhead. "Round up everyone in the Hundred-Acre Wood. We're having a meeting!"

At the meeting, Rabbit planned a Round-the-Clock Heffalump Alert.

"Night and day, day and night, we will all take turns watching for thieving Heffalumps!" Rabbit announced.

"D-dear me," whispered Piglet.

"I will track down that Heffalump," said Tigger "And when I find him, I'll bounce him and bounce him and bounce him some more. Like this!" Tigger bounced Rabbit to demonstrate.

"Dear, dear me," said Piglet.

Eeyore shook his head.

"These things always happen to me. I'm going home.
What's more, I'm not coming back until the Heffalump is
gone. Good-bye."

"Dear, oh, dear, oh, dear," Piglet said, sighing.

"Now everyone in the whole Hundred-Acre Wood is worried," thought Piglet as he watched his friends build a Heffalump Trap. "I wish I hadn't fibbed about the honey pot."

Just then Piglet had another idea.
His friends were too busy building their Heffalump Trap to
notice him leaving.

It was hard work, but Piglet dug up the pieces of the honey pot so he could take them home and try to glue them back together.

"Maybe Pooh won't notice," he thought.

As he hurried home with the pieces Piglet fell into a huge hole. Suddenly a net came down over him and alarm bells rang out.

Piglet was caught in the Heffalump Trap.

"The Heffalump! We caught him!" Rabbit shouted gleefully
when he and Pooh arrived.
"That's not a Heffalump," Pooh noticed. "That's Piglet.

"We caught a Heffalump but he turned out to be Piglet," explained Pooh when Christopher Robin came to see what was going on.

"It's my f-fault," said Piglet. "I was afraid Pooh wouldn't like me if he found out that I broke his lucky green honey pot, so I told a fib about a Heffalump.

"But that fib led to another fib. Soon all my friends in the Hundred-Acre Wood were upset," Piglet continued. "Now I know I'll never tell a fib again!"

Christopher Robin smiled. "I know what you mean," he told Piglet. "No matter how hard it is to tell the truth, it's much worse to tell a fib!"

The next day Christopher Robin helped Piglet and Pooh put the lucky green honey pot back together.

Later, Pooh and Piglet went off to pick haycorns again.

"I don't really need a lucky green honey pot," said Winnie the Pooh. "I'm already lucky to have you for my friend."

Piglet smiled. "And I am especially lucky to have you for my friend."

"Really? Do you mean it?" asked Pooh.

"I wouldn't fib," Piglet explained. "Not ever again!"